A Gift *from* **Me** *to* **You**

A Gift
from **Me**
to **You**

Tammy McDonald

Order this book online at www.trafford.com
or email orders@trafford.com

Most Trafford titles are also available at major online book retailers.

Printed in the United States of America.

ISBN: 978-1-4669-1371-4 (sc)

Library of Congress Control Number: 2012901903

Trafford rev. 03/30/2012

 www.trafford.com

North America & international
toll-free: 1 888 232 4444 (USA & Canada)
phone: 250 383 6864 ♦ fax: 812 355 4082

The Message

*A*manda stretched her legs for the last time before taking her place at the starting line. She was no stranger to the city's annual run for the Cure for Cancer.

Amanda set the timer on her watch, and placed her headphones on her head. "Runners take your mark, get . . ." Amanda held her body extremely still and waited for the start. "Bang!" Amanda shot off the line like a bullet coming out of a barrel! As she ran past the cheering crowd and made her way toward the city's country side, Amanda could feel the earth under her sneakers and could hear the breathing of the others all around her. To find her own rhythm to get through the ten miles; she reached for the cassette player on her side and pressed the play button.

"Hi baby, it's your mother. Before I begin, I just want you to know that I love you more than life itself, and no matter where you go, or what you do, take this message with you . . ."

The Surprise

*E*rika placed the last dish on the dining room table and lit the candles. As she stood back to take one last look at the table set for two, she could only smile to herself because she knew that this would be a night that she and Wesley would never forget. Looking at her watch Erika said out loud, "Oh, it's almost 5:30, I had better hurry up."

Erika quickly went back to her room and slipped into her long black silk dress, and then sat down at her vanity to apply her make-up. After combing the curls out of her hair, she put on Wesley's favorite perfume; she wanted everything to be perfect for him tonight.

Erika walked through the house to make sure that everything was in order. As she turned on the smooth jazz CD, she heard Wesley's key in the front door.

Wesley opened the door to the smooth sounds of jazz, and the aroma of dinner. He was overcome with anticipation, because he knew that Erika was just on the other side of the wall. "Baby, I'm home." Wesley said as he placed his briefcase and suit jacket on the table in the hallway.

As Erika took the small box out of the kitchen cabinet and placed it behind the centerpiece so that Wesley could not see, she called out, "I'm in here sweetheart."

Wesley walked into the dining room, and took a look at his wife and all of his senses immediately went on overload. She still had the same effect on him just like the first day he laid eyes on her! "Hello beautiful," he said taking Erika into his arms and kissing her gently on the lips. "You smell delicious, and you look breath taking." Wesley said, spreading Erika's arms out and standing back to look at her dress. "What's the occasion?"

Leading Wesley to his place at the head of the table, Erika said, "I have a surprise for you, but first, let's eat."

After dinner, Wesley pushed his plate back, "That was a wonderful dinner and a lovely surprise, and now why don't you get . . ."

"Wait a minute, I'm not quite finished with my surprise yet." said Erika reaching for the box from behind the centerpiece and placing it in front of Wesley.

Puzzled Wesley asked, "What's this?"

"Just open it." Erika said, putting interlocking fingers together and resting her chin on top. Wesley opened the box slowly, not quite sure of what he would find. He pulled back the tissue paper to find a small letter folded in half. He unfolded the letter and began to read.

I can't wait to meet you in 8 months. Love, Baby Morris

Somewhat taken back by the message, Wesley looked in the box and pulled out a baby bib that read I LOVE DADDY. Not sure if he truly comprehended what he was reading. Wesley looked over at Erika. "Is this what I think it means?" Wesley asked with tears in his eyes.

"Yes, darling, we're going to have a baby." Erika said with a glowing smile.

Wesley got up from the table and went to Erika's chair. Turning her chair around to face him, he kneeled down in front of her and placed his hands on her stomach. "Do you really mean it; is there really a little me and you in there?"

"Yes baby." Erika said caressing Wesley's chest.

Wesley gently kissed Erika's stomach and said, "Baby, it's your daddy." He then looked at his wife, and said, "Do you know how much I love you Erika?"

As tears rolled down Erika's face, she could only nod as she faintly whispered, "Yes."

Wesley then gently grabbed her face and pulled her to him and kissed her on the lips and then held her close to him. "Thank you." He whispered in her ear, "Thank you for making me the luckiest man in the world."

The next morning, Erika woke to the warm sun on her face and the smell of bacon. For a moment she lay still amazed by the life changes that she and Wesley were experiencing and how exciting it had been already; rubbing her stomach, she said out loud, "If this is a dream, please don't let me wake up."

Erika's thoughts were interrupted by the sound of Wesley's morning greeting. "Good morning Sweetie, I made you and my baby something to eat."

"Oh, how sweet, thank you!" Erika said as she propped herself up so that Wesley could set the breakfast tray down."

"Nothing is too good for my babies." Wesley said placing a piece of fresh cut fruit in Erika's mouth.

"I was thinking," Erika said as she finished chewing her fruit, "Why don't we invite everyone over tonight to tell them the news. After all, we haven't had a real open house since we moved into our new home, and we'll finally have a great come back when your mother decides to start inquiring as to why I haven't given her some grandchildren. You would think that she would protest any more grandchildren after Ebony's two terrors and Ryan's four half pint monsters! Hopefully, our children will have more brain cells than your brother and sister's demon children!"

Extremely tickled by his wife's truthful humor, Wesley said, "I hope you're right, but to tell you the truth, I'm looking forward to watching the reaction on your mother's face! I tell you, she came short of testing my sperm count herself to see if I was able to get you pregnant!" As they both laughed at the extreme pressure from both sides of their families, as he bent down to kiss his wife again, Wesley said "you're right, we have to have this party. I'll be back in 30 minutes with the groceries."

The evening was going great, Erika thought to herself as she stared at her husband from across the dinner table. Erika always loved it when all of her and Wesley's family could come together and just enjoy one another. As she looked at everyone at the table, she realized that fate brought the two families together.

There's Ryan, Wesley's twin brother who is the columnist at the same newspaper as Erika. Then there is Lola, Erika's life-long friend. Lola is who Erika always accredited as the connecting force to the whole love circle. After Erika had convinced Lola to leave her old job as a book editor and come to the Informant as the chief editor, that's when things started to come together. She and Ryan started spending lots of time together. Ryan would often accompany her and Lola to lunch at Tasties, the best chicken and rib hut in Wilson, NC. Erika could remember being tickled when she learned that Ryan and Ebony, the owner of Tasties were brother and sister. However; it was Ebony's ingenious idea and Lola's pressuring that brought Erika and Wesley together. After finally giving in, a month later, and agreeing to have Wesley join them for lunch Erika; knew that this was the man for her. It was no secret to anyone that sat at the same table that day for lunch, that Erika and Wesley craved each other. Five years later, their craving for each other continues to shine like an eternal flame.

"What are you day dreaming about, Baby Girl?" asked Erika's father, Benson.

"Oh, nothing Dad, I'm just happy that we're all together, that's all," replied Erika as she reached over and touched her father's hand.

"Well, everything was outstanding Erika. You have really out done yourself," said Wesley's mother, Mary.

Wiping her mouth with her dinner napkin Erika answered, "Well, as much as I would love to take responsibility for this delicious meal, I can't. Wesley did everything."

"Well, who would have known?" giggled Ebony as she playfully punched her brother on his forearm.

Picking up his glass and standing up from his chair Wesley replied, "I thank you for your approval, and now, if I could, I would like to take this time to share some news with all of you that I know will make you as happy as it made me when I heard it." Raising his glass he continued, "Can I get all of you to help me toast my beautiful wife?" Somewhat puzzled by this unusual request, everyone raised their glasses toward Erika. With a smile, Wesley cleared his voice to continue. "Erika, thank you for being a wonderful friend, wife, and sounding board when I've needed one; and there is no doubt in my mind that you will be a magnificent mother. I love you Erika, and thank you for making me the happiest man on the face of this earth. Here's to you, Baby."

Unable to control her emotions from her husband's surprise speech, Erika responded by throwing Wesley a kiss from across the table. "I love you too; and thank you for the love that you have and continue to give me every day."

"Wait a minute." Said Lola in disbelief, "You mean to tell me that you are . . ."

"Yes" said Erika; "we're going to have a baby. I found out on Friday. Can you imagine; for the last four months, I thought that I kept getting that virus that was going around, and I had a life growing inside me the whole time!"

"Well, I for one am glad for the two of you." Ryan said toasting his glass to both Wesley and Erika again. "Now mama and Ms. Doris won't be able to terrorize the two of you about giving them grandchildren anymore." As everyone at the table laughed, Doris, Erika's mother, could only flick her tongue at Ryan.

"Were we really that bad?" asked Mary, as she tried to catch her breath from laughing so hard.

"I'll answer that for you, son." said Benson, "Yes, between you and my wife, you two were ready to enroll those kids into a fertility clinic!"

Through all the laughter Wesley caught his wife's eyes, as he winked an eye and mouthed the words I Love You. At that very moment Erika put a gentle hand on her stomach and smiled back at her husband. Feeling the love that surrounded her, and the blessing of being able to bring life into the world, Erika knew that nothing could touch her and Wesley's happiness.

Two Weeks Later

*E*rika stood in the mirror admiring the last new outfit that she had purchased. Although she wasn't quite showing yet, her clothes were starting to be slightly tight around the waist. Placing both hands on her stomach, Erika said, "Hi there, it's mama. How are you doing in there? Did you have fun shopping with Mama today? Don't you worry; we'll have lots of time to do it once you're here."

The ringing of the telephone interrupted Erika's conversation. She walked over to the nightstand to pick up the phone. "Hello." She said in a very relaxed voice.

"Hi girl, how are you doing?" it was Lola.

"Oh, hey, I'm fine, what's up?" asked Erika as she made herself comfortable on the bed.

"I was calling to see if everything was okay. When I called you at your office the machine said that you would be gone for the rest of the day, and I was just making sure that everything was okay." said Lola in a concerned voice.

"I know who didn't check their voice mail today." Erika teased her friend as she began to take off her outfit. "I called to let you know that I was going to the mall to buy a few outfits."

"Oh, I'm sorry! I have 12 messages, and to tell you the truth, I was not motivated to take on any new tasks today." answered Lola. "Oh, by the way before I forget," Lola continued, "I still have some of my maternity clothes. If you want them, I'll drop them by later this evening after Ryan comes in from covering that high school basketball championship game."

"That would be great! Thank you, but if we're still going to our doctor's appointment tomorrow, just save yourself a trip, and I will get them tomorrow." said Erika as she looked up when she heard the front door open.

"That's a date." Lola said, "I'll pick you up at 9:00 am!"

Smiling when she saw Wesley standing in the doorway Erika answered, "I'll be ready. I'll see you tomorrow, bye." Placing the phone on the hook, Erika turned her attention to her husband. "Hi baby, how was your day?"

As Wesley walked over and bent down to kiss his wife he answered, "It was good. All the computers that I worked with cooperated, which made my job very easy. What about your day?" Wesley continued as he walked to his side of the closet to hang up his jacket and take off his tie and shoes.

Standing up to gather all the clothes that she had just purchased, she replied, "Work was unusually slow today, I covered two stories, then took the rest of the day off, so that I could go shopping." Erika said as she held up a few outfits for Wesley to see.

"I like . . . I like . . . !" said Wesley as he looked at the clothes Erika picked out. Changing the subject, Wesley asked in a more concerned voice, "Did I hear you say that you had to go to the doctor tomorrow, is everything okay?"

"Oh yeah, it's just a physical examination to make sure that everything is in place and to answer any questions that I may have. Nothing to worry about, it's just routine." Erika answered in a reassuring voice.

"Do I need to go with you?" asked Wesley. "No, it's just a physical, besides Lola has one tomorrow too, so we'll just go together." replied Erika as she slipped on her robe. "Now . . ." Erika said changing the subject completely. "What do you want for dinner?"

Walking over and grabbing his wife pulling her close to him and kissing her neck, Wesley replied, "You'll do."

"Seriously, silly," Erika said giggling at her husband's remark.

"Okay, okay, why don't you put on one of those cute outfits over there, and let me take you out to eat, and then let's come back here for desert. Wesley said winking his eye at Erika.

Smiling back at her husband she replied, "That sounds great; but just remember, desert is how we got this baby!" Erika and Wesley spent the next twenty minutes laughing and talking as they prepared for their date.

The next morning, Erika and Lola sat in the half crowded doctor's office. The two of them always enjoyed spending time together away from work; it allowed time to be friends instead of colleagues. Their friendship was special to Erika because they had been friends since kindergarten. Erika was even the godmother to her and Ryan's four children.

"I still can't believe it." said Lola as she took Erika's hand into both of hers. "You and Wesley are having a baby! You have to know how happy I am for you two. Now I get the chance to spoil my godchild niece or nephew rotten!"

"I know what you mean." Erika said with a million-dollar smile. "Now I won't have to keep stealing your children."

"Have you thought of any names yet?" asked Lola as she pointed at a list of names in the baby magazine she was looking through.

Just as Lola started calling out names, she was interrupted by the nurse. "Erika Morris the doctor will see you now."

Passing the magazine to Erika, as she stood up to walk to the back Lola replied, "Here take this with you while you're waiting, I'm finished having babies."

To Erika's surprise she had only been waiting less than ten minutes before the doctor had come in to examine her. "Hello, Erika, how have we been doing?" asked Doctor Carmichael as he quickly looked over her chart and then passed it to his nurse.

"Everything has been going just fine; I haven't had any problems so far." Erika answered as she closed the magazine and placed it in the book holder behind her.

"Well let's see," said Dr. Carmichael as he began his examination, making sure that he explained everything as he went along. Erika was very comfortable with Dr. Carmichael, she has been his patient ever since she was sixteen.

After checking Erika's throat, breathing, reflexes, breasts, cervix and baby's heartbeat, Dr. Carmichael went back to re-examine her breast. "Erika, have you experienced any tenderness in your breasts lately?"

"No, not really, I thought that the little soreness I was feeling was just from the pregnancy." answered Erika in an uncertain voice.

Helping Erika to a sitting position and stepping back from the examination table to take a seat on his stool, Dr. Carmichael said, "Erika, now I don't want you to be alarmed, but I would like you to have a mammogram done this morning. Your left breast has some lumps, and I just want to make sure that everything is okay."

Frowning slightly, and fighting hard to concentrate on what the doctor was saying Erika asked, "What's wrong, do I have cancer, what about my baby . . . ?"

Standing up and walking over to comfort Erika, Dr. Carmichael said, "The first thing that I want you to do, is to calm down. These are just tests to rule out any suspicions that I may have. Now you just sit right here while I go and arrange for the tests."

Erika couldn't help but cry after the doctor had left the room. "Is there anyone I can call for you, sweetie?" asked the nurse in a concerned voice.

Quickly wiping her tears Erika answered, "Uh, yes, Lola Morris, my sister-in-law was scheduled to see Dr. Matthew today, she should be finished now."

"I'll go check for you, Honey." said the nurse closing the door and leaving Erika all alone.

"Please don't let this be happening to me." Erika said as she put her hands on her head and began to weep. Moments later, Erika quickly lifted her head and wiped her tears when she heard the door open.

"Okay, the technician is waiting for you down the hall." said the nurse as she entered the room and closed the door behind her. "I looked for your sister-in-law in the waiting room. She's in with the doctor, so as soon as she has finished, I will have her come to this room." said the nurse as she opened the door to escort Erika down the hall.

Twenty minutes later, Erika returned to her original examining room to find Lola waiting for her.

"Hey is everything okay?" Lola asked with concern as soon as Erika walked in and closed the door behind her. For a moment, Erika was silent as she took off her doctor's gown and began to get dressed. "Lola," said Erika half dazed with tear filled eyes, "I was just examined for breast cancer."

Not quite sure if she had heard her friend correctly Lola asked in disbelief, "What are you saying . . . that you have cancer . . . ?"

"I don't know, I mean Dr. Carmichael suggested a mammogram immediately to rule out any suspicion, but . . ."

Sitting on the edge of her seat Lola reached for her purse, to pull out her cellular phone. "Has anyone called Wesley for you yet?"

"No!" Erika said in a stressed out voice. "I don't want him to know until I have the results back from Dr. Carmichael. There is no need to worry him if there's no cause to."

Empathizing that Erika was dealing with a lot, and the last thing she needed was to carry this burden alone, Lola walked over to her nervous friend who sat fully dressed on the examining table trying desperately to pull herself together. "Erika, I realize that you don't want to upset Wesley, but, if the shoe were on the other foot, wouldn't you want to know?" Besides, if the tests come back, and there are no problems then, the two of you can breathe a sigh of relief together."

Looking at her friend in desperation Erika asked, "And if the test comes back and I have cancer?"

Placing the phone in her best friend's hand Lola answered, "Then you two will be able to get a head start on how to beat this thing together."

Later That Evening

*I*t was after 4:00 pm in the evening when Wesley and Erika had returned home from the doctor's office. Wesley placed Erika's purse and all the literature that they received from the doctor's office, on the dining room table. For a moment the room was silent. It was the first time that Wesley had ever been lost for words with Erika in their entire relationship.

Sensing Wesley's discomfort, Erika cleared her voice to find an even tone. "Oh honey I almost forgot, I've got to meet a deadline for a story I've been working on. I will be back as soon as I can." Without waiting for a response from her husband, Erika hurried out of the house, and jumped into the car and drove off into the evening sunset.

When Erika finally brought the car to a stop, she found herself at her favorite quiet spot. As she looked out over the grassy hills that surrounded the small park, she found herself filled with anger. As she hit the steering wheel with her fist she could only ask out loud, "Why me? Why now?" As tears ran down her cheeks, Erika laid her head back on the seat and closed her eyes.

Fighting hard to understand what was happening to her; Erika looked down at her stomach. Through tear filled eyes she gently ran her hands across her stomach. "How are you, my sweet baby?" she said in a soft uneven voice. "Don't you worry; mama will make sure that nothing happens to you. You just hang on, and everything will be okay." she said sobbing even harder. Consumed with desperation Erika laid her head back on the seat, searching within to find the answers for the questions that continued to ricochet in her mind.

Wesley looked at the clock and paced back across the dining room to look out the window at Erika's empty parking space. Worried out of his mind, Wesley wanted nothing more than to hold his wife, and make all the pain go away. As he sat down at the dining table, he was quickly reminded of what this baby meant to both of them. As Wesley took a look at all the information that lay in front of him, his head began to ache. As long as he could remember, being a good father and husband is what he lived for. And now that God has blessed him with a baby with the woman he loved so much; how could something like this happen. "Why me" Wesley yelled in rage as the tears ran down his face. "Why does this have to happen?"

Wesley was in such deep thought that he wasn't aware that the phone was ringing. His first reaction was to let the phone ring, but remembered that Erika was out there, and she may be trying to call. Rushing over to the phone, Wesley quickly picked up the receiver. "Baby, is that you?" He said in a panicked voice.

"No, Sweetie, it's me, Mama." said a soft supporting voice on the other end. "Are you two alright?" Lola and Ryan stopped by and told me the news. Is there anything I can do?"

There was a long pause; unable to contain himself, Wesley let out a floodgate of emotions. "Mama, why mama? I did it all right!" Wesley said as he broke down to his mother. "Mama, I need . . . I need . . ."

"SHH . . . Baby, everything is going to be okay."

"Mama, can I come over, right now. I'm in no condition to be alone." cried Wesley.

"Sweetie, you know that you're always welcome here, where is Erika?" asked Mary.

Mustering up the energy to speak, Wesley said, "She needed to go. Without saying much of anything she just left."

Finding the most loving voice Mary answered in defense of her daughter-in-law. "Now Wesley, I know that you are hurting, but everyone handles news differently. Understand that Erika is feeling the same hurt that you are feeling if not worse. So you have to give her room to sort through and process everything that was just dumped on her today. Do you understand?"

Weeping even harder now, Wesley could only answer a simple, "yes."

Continuing in the same voice Mary said. "Now baby what it sounds like you need is support, so that you can be a sounding board for Erika. Now hang up the phone and wait for your brother. I sent him over to get you, and he should be there shortly, okay?"

Without another word, Wesley hung up the phone.

Where are you ?

*W*esley slowly placed the phone back on the hook, and stumbled back on the loveseat. "Erika's parents are on their way over." He said to his mother and brother. "Mom, what are we going to do, I'm so numb, and on top of all of this, I don't have a clue where my wife is. I called her office, the cell phone, and even home, but there is still no answer.

"Just give her some time Baby, she'll come around, this is just her way of trying to make some sense of all of this." said Wesley's mother as she stood over him gently stroking his hair like she used to do when he was younger.

Somewhat lost for words, Ryan asked, "Is there anything that I can do . . . I'm sorry. I can't even imagine what you must be going through." Looking up at his brother with tears in his eyes, Wesley could only shake his head. Not accustomed to seeing his older brother in such a state, Ryan wanted so badly to ease the pain for him. "Listen," Ryan said desperate to do something, "I will go out and see if she's riding around, and I will even put in a call to some of our friends down at the police station to look out for her. Don't worry Wes, we'll find her."

Overcome by emotions, Wesley attempted to say thank you, only to break down again. Touched by the sorrow that his brother was feeling, Ryan swelled with tears as he walked toward the door.

Twenty-minutes later, the ringing of the doorbell sang out through the silent house. "I'll get it" Mary said as she instantly rose to her feet and headed to the door. Taking a deep breath and trying to gain his composure the best he could, Wesley listened to see if he could make out who was at the door.

He could hear his mother's voice greeting the Browns. Wesley could feel his whole body growing numb. He instantly found himself feeling trapped like a deer caught in the headlights. All sorts of things started running through his mind. How was he going to tell his in-laws that their only child had cancer? Should he wait for Erika so that they could tell them together? Should Erika tell them alone? "Where are you?" Wesley desperately said out loud.

"Where's who?" Asked his mother-in-law as she leaned down to hug her son-in-law.

"Oh, hello, I didn't even hear the two of you come in." said Wesley quickly standing.

"It's a good thing that we're here," said Mr. Brown extending his hand. "Now you can stop talking to yourself."

For a brief moment the room was quiet as the four of them sat down. "So," Doris said clearing her throat, and pulling a list out of her purse, "I was just sitting around today, and thought that we should get a jump start on finding our little bundle of joy a name." She was just about to continue chatting when she stopped herself, "Where is Erika? I hope she is not at work at this hour! I'll tell you something we are going to have to tie her down, if she doesn't learn to rest. Wesley, baby, call her right now, so I can talk to her."

As Wesley looked at his in-laws and the list that Doris had set down, he could only cry. "Mama . . ." he uttered through his tears. Mary walked over and sat on the arm of the chair that her son was sitting in, and gently stroked his back.

Growing concerned Benson leaned forward and said, "What's going on, son, did you two get into a fight?"

"Um, no she . . ." Wesley said slowly trying to keep his voice steady. "Um . . . Erika went to the doctor today and um . . ."

"Is something wrong with the baby?" Doris said anxiously. "She . . . um, I mean . . ." Wesley said fighting desperately to find the words.

"Go on, dear" said his mother as she continued to stroke her son's back.

Leaning forward and taking a deep breath Wesley said, "Today at the doctor, Erika learned that she has breast cancer."

Not quite sure if she heard her son in law correctly, Doris echoed Wesley's words again. "Did you say breast cancer?" Too upset to speak, Wesley could only shake his head to confirm. "Oh, Dear God, Benson, our baby has cancer!" Doris said as she collapsed into her husband's arms and began to sob out loud.

Trying to make sense of the news himself, Benson asked in disbelief over his wife's crying, "Are you sure that's what the doctor said, son?"

"Yes sir." Wesley said wiping the running tears from his face.

"Where is she now?" Benson continued looking around to see if he saw her.

"I don't know." Wesley said in a whisper. "After we returned from the doctor, she just turned around and walked out of the door, she didn't say where she was going."

"Ryan has gone out to look for her and we called her office; and they will call us as soon as she steps foot in the door." said Mary in an empathetic manner. "Please, wait here with us; I'm sure someone will spot her soon." Mary continued as she walked over to comfort Doris who was now crying uncontrollably.

Standing up from the sofa, Benson took his keys from his pocket. "I can't just sit here, I have to go and look too."

"Can I go with you?" Wesley asked as he rose to his feet. I can't just sit here any longer."

"Come on, son." Benson said after hearing the desperate plea from his son-in-law. Benson turned to his wife and gently wiped away her tears. "Now Sweetie, listen; everything is going to be okay, we will all get through this." Overcome with emotion, Doris could only nod her head as she turned and walked over and stood looking out over the rose garden in Mary's backyard.

"Don't worry." said Mary as she walked Benson and her son to the front door. "I will see to it that Doris is fine, you just find Erika, and bring her back safe and sound. Take God with you son, and I'll be praying for you." She whispered as she hugged her son.

When Erika had finally brought herself to a calm state of mind, she slowly stepped out of her truck to take in all of the silent beauty that surrounded her. Erika walked down to sit on the steep flowery hill overlooking the pond. Gently touching the petals of the violets, she could remember the first time her father brought her here, she was only six years old. She had made a wish on a falling star that she could have her very own special wishing well. The next day, her father woke her up early and told her that he had a surprise for her. Erika could recall being so excited as she sat looking out of the window as her father drove her to her surprise. When they had finally arrived, her father told her to close her eyes. Erika managed to muster up a small smile when she remembered how tight she closed her eyes as her father lifted her from the car seat and carried her to the very spot she was now sitting. Erika could still hear her father's voice as if it were yesterday when he said; "now Princess, open your eyes."

"It's beautiful Daddy, but where are we." Erika remembered asking her father.

"It's your very own wishing well," her father said as he picked her up and carried her all the way down the hill to the small pond. Now he said as he passed her one shiny penny. "Close your eyes and make a wish." From that day on, whenever Erika needed to get away, to think, make decisions or to just make a wish, she would always find her way back to her magic pond.

Benson and Wesley had been riding around for two hours in silence. They checked all the places they thought Erika might have gone. "Where in the world could she be?" Wesley finally spoke out half-frustrated, and half-worried. "She's not home, your house, work, the mall, at the restaurant, or the hospital; no where! It's like she just vanished into thin air."

"That's it!" shouted Benson as he hit his fist on the steering wheel and began to smile. Quickly turning the car around in the middle of the road, Benson murmured, "She has to be there."

"Be where?" Wesley asked confused, but hopeful.

"Her special place," Benson said with confidence. "I took her there when she was only six, and every time she is worried about something she goes there. I will bet my life that this is where we will find our little princess."

As Wesley sat staring out of the window, looking at the beautiful scenery, he couldn't help but to think about what his mother said as he was leaving. 'Take God with you.'

Just as Wesley closed his eyes and began to pray, he heard his father in law shout, "and there's her truck." Wesley opened his eyes and looked around at the breath taking view. "Where are we?" he asked in a mystified voice.

"Erika's wishing-well." Benson said as he opened the car door and stepped out. Wesley began to step out and follow his father-in-law down to Erika who was sitting still by the pond. Losing all of his nerve, he looked desperately at Benson who was waiting for him. With Wesley's look telling it all, Benson asked, "Would it be okay if I go see how she's doing first?"

Feeling temporarily relieved by the request, Wesley managed to muster up the words, "Yes sir, I'll wait right here."

Benson felt himself rushing to his daughter. All he wanted to do was pick her up in his arms and to kiss her to make all the pain go away, but he knew that it would take more than just a kiss to relieve her anguish. No matter how much love he had to give, it couldn't possibly take her cancer away. As he reached the bottom of the hill where Erika was sitting, he reached into his pocket and pulled out a penny before sitting down next to his daughter. "Have you made a wish yet?" he asked as he held out his hand with the penny in it.

Exhausted from crying, Erika looked up at her father. "Daddy," she said falling into his arms weeping. "Why did this have to happen? Why now?"

"Oh Baby!" Benson replied trying to keep his voice from cracking. As he held his daughter tightly, he could only say as the tears came rushing down his face like a waterfall. "Please, Father, Don't take our only baby, please!" After a moment, Benson pulled Erika back. With tears still trickling down from his eyes, "Don't worry we are going to get through this. We just have to pray and stay strong." he said wiping the tears that paraded down his daughter's face. "Baby, you're not in this alone."

Erika looked up to see Wesley kneeling behind her. "Oh Wes, looking away half embarrassed. "I'm so sorry!"

Realizing that Wesley and Erika needed some time to be alone, he took his daughter's hands into both of his and gently kissed her fingers. "I will let everyone know that you're safe." As he rose to his feet and turned to leave, he simply nodded at Wesley and placed one hand on his shoulder and gently gripped it.

Once alone, Wesley sat down behind Erika spreading his legs on either side of her and gently pulled her back toward him. For a moment there was silence as he caressed her hair. Overwhelmed with joy to simply to have his wife back in his arms safe and sound,

Wesley whispered in her ear, "I love you Erika, and we are going to make it through this okay." Like a security blanket, Erika wrapped her husband's arms around her tighter and closed her eyes.

"Wesley," she said in a faint whisper, "I'm sorry to have taken the happiest moment in your life and shattered it with such horrible news."

Disturbed by Erika's way of thinking, Wesley turned her around to face him. "Now Erika you have to know that there is no reason to be sorry that you're sick. The happiest day in my life is the day that I met you. Yes, having a baby added to my already beautiful life that we shared, but if having children of our own wasn't in the plans for us, then that is something that I can live with as long as I have you in my world.

"But Wesley . . . ," Erika replied, that's all that we have been trying to do for so long; have a baby, and now that we have finally been able to conceive, this has to happen." Turning back around and leaning back on her husband, Erika said, "I just always wanted this moment to be perfect. Now instead of trying to find names for our miracle baby, we have to determine if we should proceed with this pregnancy."

Truly realizing what obstacles lay ahead, Wesley fought hard to hide the overwhelming hurt that consumed him. "Right now at this very moment the only thing I want to concentrate on is making sure that you're okay. I can't reiterate this enough, Baby; you are not in this alone, and whatever you need, know that I'm here for you."

"All I need right now," said Erika nuzzling her face in her husband's neck, is for you to hold me." As the two of them sat watching the sunset in silence, they both knew the road that lay before them would be challenging, but trying to keep their emotions and mental state stable would be an even bigger challenge.

The Feud

*W*esley brought the truck to a stop in front of his mother's house. "My goodness, is this an early family reunion?" Erika asked as she looked at the crowded driveway.

"Everyone has been worried about you." Wesley said reaching over and grabbing his wife's hand.

"I didn't mean to make everyone worry . . . I just needed some time to clear my head." said Erika.

Stepping out from his side of the truck and walking around to open Erika's door and helping her out. "Erika," he said wrapping his arms around her and pulling her close so that he could see her brown eyes dancing in the moon. "I know that you are a strong woman, in fact, you have to be one of the strongest women I know, but you have to know that you are not in this alone; we are not in this alone. Inside of that house, God has blessed us with a host of people who love and support us. We are not walking down this dark road alone."

Erika took a deep breath and smiled as she caressed the wavy locks at the nape of her husband's neck. "Thank you." she said as she leaned over to kiss Wesley gently on his lips.

"Why?" Wesley asked with a confused frown on his face. "For helping me to see how truly blessed we are, even at our darkest hour!"

"Now, promise me one thing." Wesley said taking both of Erika's hands into his and gently leading her up the driveway toward the house.

"What's that?" Erika asked with a half smile.

"Promise me that you will still see all of these people as blessings to us even after we leave here." Wesley chuckled as he unlocked the door to the chattering voices of adults and laugher of little voices running about.

"Hello everyone, we're back." Wesley called as he closed the door and walked into the living room where everyone was talking.

"Oh! My baby!" Doris cried rising from her seat and racing to embrace her daughter. "Are you alright, Honey?" I've been worried about you. Here, come over and sit down." Doris said in a half relieved, but anxious tone of voice

"I'm okay, Mom." Erika said trying to reassure her mother, while she accommodated her wish to sit down. "Everyone really, I'm okay, I just needed some time to make sense of all the news, and try to figure out my next move; but thanks to a great friend, I realize that I have all of you to help me through this." Erika said trying to choke back the tears for the worried faces that she looked at.

For a moment the room was silent as everyone tried to find something to say. Breaking the silence, Ryan asked half nervous, "So . . . what did the doctor say?"

Not wanting Erika to have to shoulder all of the questions from everyone, Wesley cleared his voice, "Well, we . . . have several things to consider. Right now, Erika's cancer is more advanced than the doctor had hoped, but the doctors are sure that with aggressive treatment, the chances of getting all of the cancer will be successful."

"That's good, right?" Ryan asked in a hopeful voice.

"Yes, it is for me." Erika said. "But for the baby, it will mean that I will have to terminate this pregnancy." she continued trying to remain strong,

"So, when is the procedure scheduled?" asked her mother in a concerned voice.

"Well," Erika replied, "that's what I have been fighting with all day. I've been waiting for years to get pregnant and to know that we have come this far for nothing . . ."

"Not for nothing, Sweetheart, for your life." interrupted Doris. "Now don't forget, there are millions of children out there that need a home."

"Mother," Erika cut her short, "I have dreamt of having children of my own for years, and now that I'm pregnant, I'm not just willing to lie on a table and have a 'procedure' done!" said Erika, somewhat frustrated by her mother's lack of sensitivity.

"Well, what did the doctor say?" Benson cut in to try to stop an argument between his wife and daughter.

Taking a deep breath, Erika said, "I have taken great care of myself, so there is a small chance that I will be able to deliver the baby and then have the doctors go in and remove the cancer from my breast."

"Well, isn't there anyway that they can go in and get the cancer now, without disturbing the fetus?" Lola asked trying to find a helpful solution.

"We wished that it were that easy." Wesley said, gently massaging his wife's shoulders as he spoke. "Because of the medication used before surgery and the chemo treatments used after surgery, there is no way the baby would be strong enough to survive."

"So how long will you have to wait after you have the baby to get the cancer removed?" asked Mary.

"Within days of the delivery, I will be able to have the surgery." answered Erika.

"Wait a minute," Doris called out in a half anxious voice. "You mean you are actually going to consider trying to have this baby?"

Not sure if she had enough nerves to stand up to her mother, Erika looked down at the floor like a grade school child as she fought to find the words to answer her mother. Before she could answer she heard, "With all due respect Doris," asked Mary in an empathetic voice, "Don't you think that this decision should be made by Erika and Wesley?"

Literally yelling at the top of her voice and startling everyone, Doris pronounced, "Mary, you can just keep your narrow minded comments to yourself! Unlike you, Erika is my only child, so after, her, I have no more children! If that means she has to terminate this baby to save her own life; then so be it!"

"Baby, please!" Benson said attempting to calm down his wife.

"No, Benson, she has children to spare, and it seems that she cares more about giving her son a baby rather than Erika's well-being."

"Now you wait one minute!" snapped Wesley at his irate mother in law. "Before you go around tossing your misplaced . . ."

"Son, please!" Mary cried out stopping Wesley from confronting or disrespecting his mother in law. Rising to her feet Mary exclaimed. "Doris Brown, if you think that for one minute that my interest is only geared around pleasing my son, then your head is the one that has been stuffed in a tube. The only thing that I was trying to point out was . . ."

"Stop it, you hear me, just stop it!" yelled Erika with tears running down her face as she stood up and started backing up towards the entrance of the living room with her hands pushing back her hair. "If this is everyone's idea of helping; then, NO THANK YOU!" She said as she made her way to the front door leaving everyone speechless.

The Discussion

*W*esley turned the key and quietly entered the dark house. He wasn't sure what state Erika would be in after the family madness she had just endured. Following the sound of the low jazz music coming from the family room, Wesley walked in to find Erika curled up on the chaise in the corner.

"Erika." He called out as he made his way over to his wife in the dimly lit room. Lifting her chin off of her raised knees, Erika looked over toward her husband. As Wesley sat down and embraced his wife, he said, "Are you okay? I'm so sorry that you had to endure what happened this evening."

"No," said Erika putting her head into Wesley's muscular chest. "I'm sorry, I shouldn't have overreacted. It was just that one minute I felt confident to stand up and endure all the questions and comments. Then everyone started to talk about death; and my personal interest, my mental and emotional systems just shut down and all of a sudden, I felt like I was in a lion's den at dinner time. I needed to escape." Sitting up and wiping the tears from her face she continued, "But mostly, I'm sorry for leaving you there to endure and bear everything."

Gently kissing his wife on the forehead and hugging her tightly he said, "Don't you worry about me, I was only bitten once." As they both giggled, Wesley stood up and reached down to help his wife stand up. "I tell you what; there is obviously a lot that we have to talk about and many decisions that we have to make quickly. Why don't you go take a shower, and I will fix one of my famous late-night snacks and we'll meet back here to sort everything out."

Realizing that this was the first civil conversation that she would be having all day about what was happening, she replied, "Okay, give me 20 minutes."

Two hours later, Wesley and Erika had listed and discussed every pro and con. Despite all of their efforts, they were still unable to come to a joint decision. Exhausted and unable to discuss anything further, Erika struggled to sound normal as she said, "It's getting late and it's been one long emotional day. I think that tomorrow will be the same, do you mind if I turn in?"

"Sure thing." replied Wesley in an unusual murmur. "I'll come to bed as soon as I finish putting our snacks away."

Wesley had finished cleaning the kitchen and turned to put away the remaining food in the refrigerator when he saw the note that Erika had given him the night she surprised him with the news:

I can't wait to meet you in 8 months. Love, Baby Morris

Wesley took the note from under the magnet and sat down at the kitchen table. As he stared at the note, he rubbed his fingers across the word Daddy. Tears began to cloud the words on the note as he murmured to himself. *All my life all, I've ever wanted was to just be happy, and nothing more. I found that happiness with Erika and together we created even more happiness, and now I have to give it all up? No, I can't! Don't take my wife, don't take my baby, take me instead.*

Unable to sleep in fear that something would happen to Erika and he wouldn't be awake to help her, Wesley sat on the floor in the corner of their room watching her sleep. While she slept, his mother's words ran through his head again. 'Take God with you.' With his back against the wall, Wesley knew that God was the only answer. With his hands folded together he bowed his head and began to pray a silent prayer. Erika opened her eyes the next morning to her husband's tired eyes.

"Good morning" Wesley said, quickly standing to his feet and coming to the bed with Erika.

Propping herself up on the pillow, she said, "You look tired, baby, didn't you sleep at all?"

Rubbing his eyes and stretching Wesley responded, "No, I spent time with God, just asking him to watch over you and our baby." For a moment there was silence as Wesley laid his head in Erika's lap looking up at her.

Stroking Wesley's hair Erika replied, "With your prayers and my prayers, God is bound to hear us, and I have faith that he is going to help us get through our decision."

Embracing
Every Moment

*E*rika folded the soft pink blanket and placed it over the crib in the newly decorated nursery. Sitting in the white glide rocker, she found herself overjoyed with how smoothly everything had come together. Looking at the framed ultrasound picture, Erika said out loud as she caressed the small image "My sweet baby, I can't wait to see you in your new room, I can imagine years of fun doing tea parties and dress up in here . . ." Erika stopped short when she saw Wesley standing in the doorway with a video camera. "What are you doing, Silly Boy?" Erika asked, holding up a hand to shield her face.

"I am capturing every beautiful moment you have." Wesley said as he walked closer to her.

"Well, in that case . . .", Erika said, reaching for the pink blanket that she had just folded wrapping it around her shoulders, "I am ready for my close up, Mr. Deville!"

Laughing at Erika's striking poses, Wesley said, "If this is any indication of what our daughter will be, then I had better get more recording tapes."

Standing up from the rocker, Erika said, "Just make sure that you save enough for the shower tonight."

Turning off the camera, Wesley looked at his wife and said, "Are you sure that you're up to this? Remember the doctor said that you shouldn't over do it."

"Yes, dear, how hard can it be to open great gifts and eat food? Those are two things that I have always enjoyed. Besides, everyone has gone through so much to put this together for us."

"Okay", said Wesley, "but the first sign that I see that you are getting tired, I am pulling the plug."

"So, that means you are staying?" Erika asked as she walked to the closet to place the blanket with the rest.

"I hope that you didn't think that I was going to let you eat up all the cake without me?" Wesley said as he walked over, kissed wife and gently caressed her stomach. "Besides, I already asked my mom to make her spinach dip and your mom to make her deviled eggs."

Laughing at the husband's boyish charm, Erika responded shaking her head, "What am I going to do with you?"

Later that evening, Erika sat and took in the moment; her family and friends were all gathered around, laughing, eating, playing games, and enjoying each other. Although Erika was worn out from the evening, she refused to show it. This was the first time in a long time that everyone around her had let their guards down and not handled her with kitten gloves.

"Have you had enough to eat?" asked Lola, snapping a picture of her friend gazing at all of her guests.

"Yes, I am stuffed, can't you tell?" Erika asked rubbing her stomach and giggling.

Sitting down next to Erika, Lola started into her investigative questioning, "How are you feeling?"

Rolling her eyes, Erika stated, "Yes dear, we are both fine, why wouldn't we be? We have had great food, great gifts, and outstanding company."

"Ok," Lola said, through curled lips, "mom is not here, so how are you *truly* doing."

Smiling at her best friend, she could only pop her hand. Erika could always appreciate how her friend could read her mind and force her to disclose what the true story is. "Well if you must know, it has been somewhat of a relief to have everyone around me relax and just enjoy themselves today. This has been an extremely stressful few months for everyone and to have to watch everyone worry all the time has been hard for me to see."

Validating Erika's feelings, Lola stated, "I can see how you could feel that way, but, Erika, you have to know that we love you and there is nothing that we wouldn't do for you to make sure that you and my little godchild are safe."

"I know," said Erika, "but I just hate to have everyone make such a fuss over me." Erika couldn't get the words out of her mouth, before she heard . . .

"Are you ok, Sweetie, do you need to wrap up?"

Smiling like the cat who ate the mouse, Erika responded to her mother-in-law, "I am fine, I am having such fun, I could use some more of your spinach dip and crackers though."

"Sure thing, Darling, I will be right back," said her mother-in-law, as she raced to toward the kitchen.

"See what I mean?" Erika said as she looked over at Lola.

"Just go with it for the next 4 months, look at this way; you have maids at your beck and call." Lola said, as she tried to find a way for her friend to get use to her new reality.

"Oh in that case, can you rub my feet?" teased Erika.

Returning the joke, Lola said, "This is my day off."

For the next few hours, the two friends spent the evening enjoying each other's company and making plans to be ageless parents.

No Regrets

*E*rika sat in the hospital bed holding Amanda, her baby girl. "Now baby, I want you to be good for Daddy, okay?" Erika said as she smiled at the cooing bundle in her arms.

"We will be taking you down in 20 minutes, okay, Mrs. Morris." said the nurse as she changed Erika's IV bag.

"Thank you." said Erika. Once the nurse had gone, Erika passed Amanda to Wesley. Erika looked up at all of her loved ones. "Well," she said clearing her voice, "this is it."

"You're going to be fine," Ebony said, reaching over to touch her sister-in-law's leg.

"I know I will," said Erika, "but I just need to let all of you know, that despite what happens, I have no regrets, and every time I look down at Amanda, I'm sure of it. Lola and Ebony, I want you two to be Amanda's godmothers. Make sure she knows and sees your strength as women."

Trying to find the same amount of strength as Erika, they both sound out together, "Okay."

"Ryan . . ."

"Don't!" Ryan said, refusing to acknowledge Erika's critical situation.

"No, Ryan, listen" Erika said, "let's not pretend that everything is okay. My chances are less than 50%, so listen. I want you to be Amanda's godfather, and a sounding board for Wesley. Whenever Wesley can't be there, I want you to be there okay, you promise?" Choking back tears he nodded.

Turning to Mary, Erika said, "Mother Mary, be there for Wesley. When parenting gets too overwhelming, remind him of the joys of parenthood, okay?"

Reaching in her purse for a tissue Mary nodded, "God bless you, baby."

Turning to her parents Erika extended her hands and placed them over both of theirs. "Mom, Dad," she said, in a strong voice, "Thank you, for giving me life, and teaching me to enjoy it every day. It's because of your spiritual guidance and unconditional love, I am able to look forward with no regrets and for that, I will always love you both. Promise me that you will love Amanda like you have loved me, and make sure that she gets to see my special place okay, Daddy?"

Weeping, her father reached over and kissed her, "I will Princess."

"I will, too, Baby" her mother whispered picking up her daughter's hand and kissing it. "You are truly a wonderful mother, do you know that?"

"I learned from the best." said Erika, as she reached over and gently kissed her mother.

Now taking a deep breath, "That wasn't so bad. Now I need to talk with Wesley. Can one of you take Amanda for us?" Passing the baby to Lola, Wesley stood back while everyone took a moment to kiss Erika and wish her well.

Once alone, Wesley turned to Erika, "Do you know how much I admire and love you?"

"I love you too." said Erika, "Now, we don't have much time so listen. There's so much I want to say, and need to say to you. Above all, I just want to thank you for coming into my life and filling it with joy every day. Take that with you. Never let our daughter forget about me, make sure that she knows how much I love her. Show her the pictures, and let her listen to the tapes. Take time to enjoy her and never forget that she's my gift to you."

Reaching over to kiss his wife, Wesley said, "Erika Morris, I love you so much, and after all this is over, I'm going to take you on a vacation, anywhere you want to go."

"I'm going to hold you to that!" Erika said as she pressed her face against his.

The faint tap at the door interrupted them, "It's time." Said the nurse as she and two orderlies prepared to move her.

"I'll be right here when you return." Wesley said kissing his wife again.

Hours later, Wesley was summoned by the nurse to come to a conference room. Too afraid to handle any news alone, he turned to Erika's parents, "Will you come with me please?"

"Sure son." Benson said, rising with his wife by his side. Passing the baby to his mother, Wesley turned to join the Brown's as they went down the hall to the windowless conference room. Minutes later, Wesley reappeared

"What is it?" Lola said, as she looked at Wesley's expressionless face. He walked over and reached for Amanda. Sitting down and studying her little face, he said in disbelief, "She didn't make it."

As everyone in the room began to weep, Wesley bent down to kiss his daughter, "It's just you and me. When you get older, I will tell you about the very special gift your mother gave to both of us."

The Test of Endurance

*P*rayer and faith, the two things that continued to be the foundation for the Morris family, and Amanda knew that it was the basis of her existence for twenty-six years. As she rounded the last 60 yards of her marathon, she could hear the cheers and encouragement from all of her loved ones through her headphones.

As she crossed the finish line, she realized that this race was more than a test of endurance; it was a test of strength. A lesson her mother passed on.

"My dearest Amanda, you must always remember, life ends the day we're born, and it will be important that you live everyday to the fullest, because life is a gift, and this is my gift to you. I love you, baby girl, and I always will."

As Amanda came to a stop, she pulled off her headphones. She took the cassette player from her waist and caressed her mother's message. She held the cassette player close to her heart and looked up to the beautiful sky. "I love you too."

As she closed her eyes to take in the cool breeze that blew over her sweaty face, she heard a tiny voice, "Mama, Who are you talking to?" Amanda turned to see her loving husband, two children and her father.

Reaching down and picking up her four-year old, she replied, "To my angel, Sweetie . . . to my angel."

Printed in the United States
By Bookmasters